This book is to be returned on or befor
the last date stamped below.

This Little Tiger book
belongs to:

_____

_____

_____

_____

_____

To Rich and to Pa
~*H.P.*

For Eve
~*N.R.*

LITTLE TIGER PRESS
1 The Coda Centre, 189 Munster Road,
London SW6 6AW
www.littletigerpress.com
This paperback edition published 2002
First published in Great Britain 2001
Text © 2001 Helen Peacock
Illustrations © 2001 Neil Reed
Helen Peacock and Neil Reed have asserted their right
to be identified as the author and illustrator of this work
under the Copyright, Designs and Patents Act, 1988
Printed in Belgium
All rights reserved • ISBN 1 85430 739 8
1 3 5 7 9 10 8 6 4 2

The Strong Little Tree

by Helen Peacock
illustrated by Neil Reed

LITTLE TIGER PRESS
London

At the edge of a wood
stood a grand old oak tree.
In autumn the sun shone, the
rain fell and the wind blew a little.
One day, an acorn dropped from
its branch on to the ground.

A squirrel came bobbing out of the wood and saw the acorn. She had already eaten plenty that day so she picked it up and carried it away into the field, where she buried it for eating in the winter.

The winter came.
Sometimes the sun shone, but more
often the rain fell and the wind blew.

Jack Frost danced in the early
morning and sprinkled magic
ice dust all over the field.
The squirrel dug for nuts and
acorns, but the acorn from the
grand old oak tree stayed
snug in the ground.

The spring came.
The sun shone,
the rain fell, and
sometimes the
wind blew.

The acorn split
open. It pushed
up a tiny shoot,
and it pushed
down a tiny root.

Two little leaves,
shiny orangy brown,
grew at the top of
the shoot. They
turned fresh green
in the sunshine.

All around the little shoot the
grass grew long and tall. Sheep
grazed in the field and nibbled
at the grass, then moved on.

Cows pulled at the grass with their thick tongues
and their heavy feet trampled the ground, then they,
too, moved on. Hidden in the grass the little acorn
shoot grew into a tiny sapling.

Two seasons passed.
The sun shone . . .

the rain fell . . .

the wind blew . . .

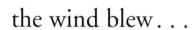

and Jack Frost
danced.

The little sapling grew a few more leaves each season, and the stem became just a little taller and a little thicker than the year before.

Under the ground the root of the sapling branched out and pushed down a little deeper and firmer into the soil.

One spring a sheep nibbled the bark of the sapling and damaged it. Another one nibbled at the leaves and broke the growing tip. But although the sapling was small and thin, it was strong. New bark grew on the tiny trunk and two new shoots grew out from the damaged tip.

That autumn, the sun was often hidden behind the clouds.
The rain beat down heavily. One night the wind howled
and gusted and whooshed in and out and around the wood.

It suddenly swirled up, fierce and angry, and blew straight at the grand old oak, then roared away.

There was a crack and a cracking and a snap
and a snapping, and a creak and a creaking,
and with a mighty heave, the ancient, rotten
roots of the old tree were torn out of the wet soil.
CRASH! With a terrible tearing, the
big oak tree thumped to the ground.

In the morning the wind was still, the rain had stopped and the sun shone weakly through the mist. In the field beside the wood lay the grand old oak tree, its great thick trunk sad and sideways. Broken branches lay all around. Where the great tree had stood for hundreds of years there was now a gaping hole.

Beside the hole the torn roots pointed to the sky. Hidden under the leaves and twigs in the field was the little oak sapling.

Men drove up with a tractor and trailer and cut off
the branches and the trunk of the old oak tree.
They threw the dead branches, thin twigs and rotten
roots into a pile in the open field. Their heavy boots
trampled to and fro around the little sapling. The men
set fire to the jagged pile of rotten wood. All that was
left of the mighty tree was a circle of white ash. But in
the field, the little oak sapling was alive and growing.

Over the years the little oak
tree grew taller and taller and
broader and broader, high above
the grass and the nibbling sheep
and the trampling cows.

Birds built their nests in
the forks of the branches
and hundreds of caterpillars
feasted on the leaves of
the new oak tree.

Each spring and summer the sun shone, and the rain fell, and in the autumn acorns tumbled to the ground. Then one autumn a jay flew out of the wood, picked up an acorn in her beak and buried it in the field nearby. And there it lay, snug in the ground, until the following spring . . .

when a tiny shoot appeared, which later grew into a strong little tree.

For information regarding any other titles
or for our full catalogue, please contact:

Little Tiger Press
1 The Coda Centre
189 Munster Road
London SW6 6AW, UK

Telephone: 020 7385 6333
Fax: 020 7385 7333
e-mail: info@littletiger.co.uk

or alternatively please visit our website:

www.littletigerpress.com